By
Anthony Tallarico

Copyright © 1992 Kidsbooks, Inc. and Anthony Tallarico
7004 N. California Avenue
Chicago, IL 60645

ISBN: 0-8317-4679-3

This edition is published in 1992 by SMITHMARK Publishers, Inc.,
16 East 32nd Street, New York, N.Y. 10016

SMITHMARK books are available for bulk purchase for sales promotion and premium use.
For details write or telephone the Manager of Special Sales, SMITHMARK Publishers, Inc.,
16 East 32nd Street, New York, N.Y. 10016 (212) 532-6600

Manufactured in the United States of America

Welcome to Creepy Castle, the castle that was never built. One moonless, creepy night it just appeared! Enter at your own risk! But first, find the following things hidden in this picture.

- ☐ Airplane
- ☐ Anchor
- ☐ Automobile
- ☐ Axe
- ☐ Bottle
- ☐ Broom
- ☐ Chair
- ☐ Clown's face
- ☐ Coffeepot
- ☐ Cup

- ☐ Duck
- ☐ Fire hydrant
- ☐ Fish
- ☐ Football
- ☐ Fork
- ☐ Hammer
- ☐ Heart
- ☐ Hockey stick
- ☐ Ice-cream cone
- ☐ Key

- ☐ Kite
- ☐ Paintbrush
- ☐ Pencil
- ☐ Ring
- ☐ Sailboat
- ☐ Screwdriver
- ☐ Star
- ☐ Toothbrush

WELCOME

Racing through a partly open curtain, our friends enter the room of a famous monster star who's hidden all kinds of things. Can you find them?

- ☐ Automobile
- ☐ Axe
- ☐ Basket
- ☐ Bat
- ☐ Bird
- ☐ Bone
- ☐ Candle
- ☐ Cups (2)
- ☐ Elephant
- ☐ Fish
- ☐ Flower
- ☐ Guitar
- ☐ Hammer
- ☐ Heart
- ☐ Igloo
- ☐ Kangaroo
- ☐ Mermaid
- ☐ Mitten
- ☐ Moon face
- ☐ Mouse
- ☐ Party hat
- ☐ Pencil
- ☐ Rabbit
- ☐ Sailboat
- ☐ Star
- ☐ Toothbrush
- ☐ Tugboat
- ☐ Whale

Now there's a weird sight — a headless knight! Could he be related to the headless horseman of Sleepy Hollow?

Before going on, find these hidden pictures.

- ☐ Baseball bat
- ☐ Book
- ☐ Bottle
- ☐ Chicken
- ☐ Cow's head
- ☐ Cupcake
- ☐ Duck
- ☐ Eagle's head
- ☐ Ear of corn
- ☐ Envelope
- ☐ Feather
- ☐ Fish
- ☐ Fishhook
- ☐ Frog
- ☐ Ghost
- ☐ Hot dog
- ☐ Key
- ☐ Paper clip
- ☐ Pea pod
- ☐ Saw
- ☐ Shoe
- ☐ Slice of bread
- ☐ Sock
- ☐ Toothbrush
- ☐ Turtle
- ☐ Umbrella
- ☐ Wheelbarrow

What lurks beneath this new knight's hood? Is he a handsome hero or another creepy creature? Before you turn the page to find out, look for the following hidden pictures.

☐ Arrow
☐ Astronaut
☐ Banana
☐ Brush
☐ Cactus
☐ Carrot
☐ Crab
☐ Electric guitar
☐ Fish

☐ Heart
☐ Helicopter
☐ Hot dog
☐ Ice-cream cone
☐ Invisible knight
☐ Key
☐ Kite
☐ Magnet
☐ Parachute

☐ Pelican
☐ Rocket ship
☐ Sailboat
☐ Skis
☐ Star
☐ Teapot
☐ Toothbrush
☐ Truck
☐ Turtle

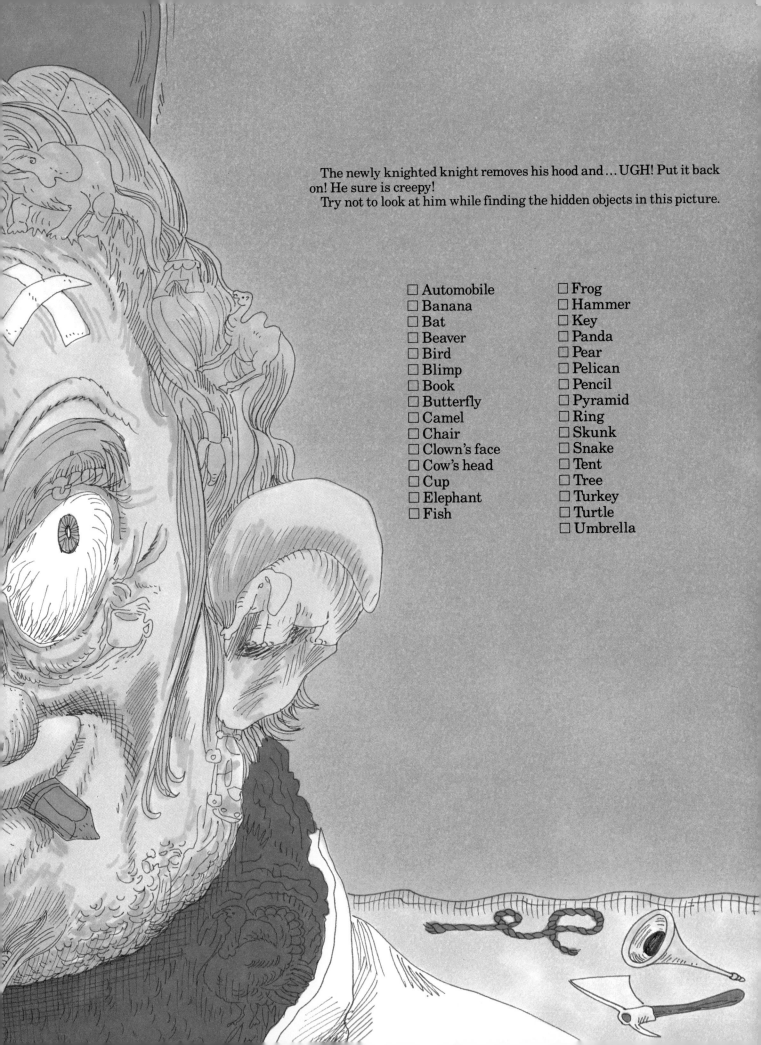

The newly knighted knight removes his hood and … UGH! Put it back on! He sure is creepy!
Try not to look at him while finding the hidden objects in this picture.

☐ Automobile
☐ Banana
☐ Bat
☐ Beaver
☐ Bird
☐ Blimp
☐ Book
☐ Butterfly
☐ Camel
☐ Chair
☐ Clown's face
☐ Cow's head
☐ Cup
☐ Elephant
☐ Fish

☐ Frog
☐ Hammer
☐ Key
☐ Panda
☐ Pear
☐ Pelican
☐ Pencil
☐ Pyramid
☐ Ring
☐ Skunk
☐ Snake
☐ Tent
☐ Tree
☐ Turkey
☐ Turtle
☐ Umbrella

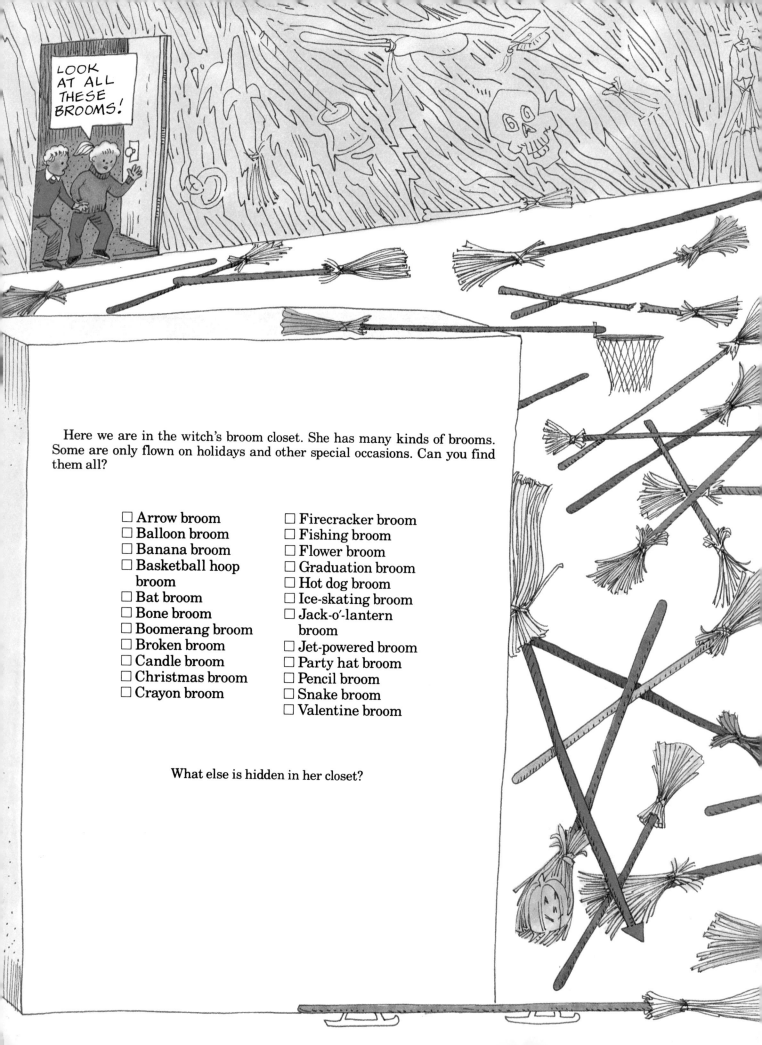

LOOK AT ALL THESE BROOMS!

Here we are in the witch's broom closet. She has many kinds of brooms. Some are only flown on holidays and other special occasions. Can you find them all?

☐ Arrow broom
☐ Balloon broom
☐ Banana broom
☐ Basketball hoop broom
☐ Bat broom
☐ Bone broom
☐ Boomerang broom
☐ Broken broom
☐ Candle broom
☐ Christmas broom
☐ Crayon broom
☐ Firecracker broom
☐ Fishing broom
☐ Flower broom
☐ Graduation broom
☐ Hot dog broom
☐ Ice-skating broom
☐ Jack-o'-lantern broom
☐ Jet-powered broom
☐ Party hat broom
☐ Pencil broom
☐ Snake broom
☐ Valentine broom

What else is hidden in her closet?

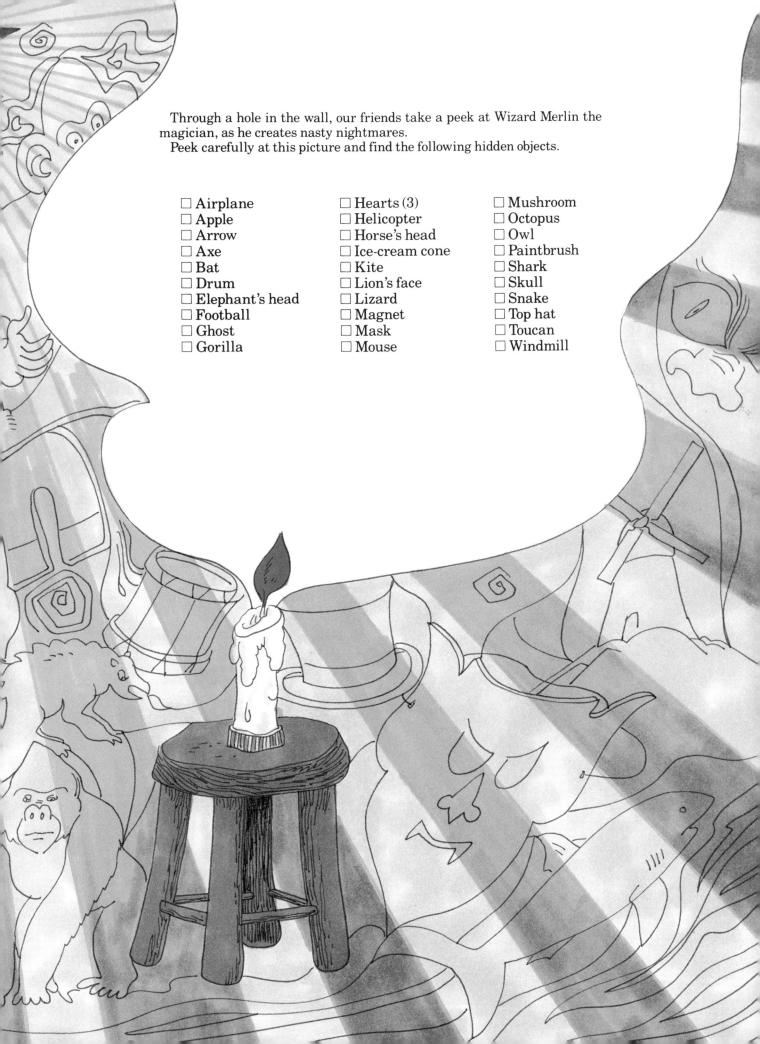

Through a hole in the wall, our friends take a peek at Wizard Merlin the magician, as he creates nasty nightmares.

Peek carefully at this picture and find the following hidden objects.

- ☐ Airplane
- ☐ Apple
- ☐ Arrow
- ☐ Axe
- ☐ Bat
- ☐ Drum
- ☐ Elephant's head
- ☐ Football
- ☐ Ghost
- ☐ Gorilla
- ☐ Hearts (3)
- ☐ Helicopter
- ☐ Horse's head
- ☐ Ice-cream cone
- ☐ Kite
- ☐ Lion's face
- ☐ Lizard
- ☐ Magnet
- ☐ Mask
- ☐ Mouse
- ☐ Mushroom
- ☐ Octopus
- ☐ Owl
- ☐ Paintbrush
- ☐ Shark
- ☐ Skull
- ☐ Snake
- ☐ Top hat
- ☐ Toucan
- ☐ Windmill

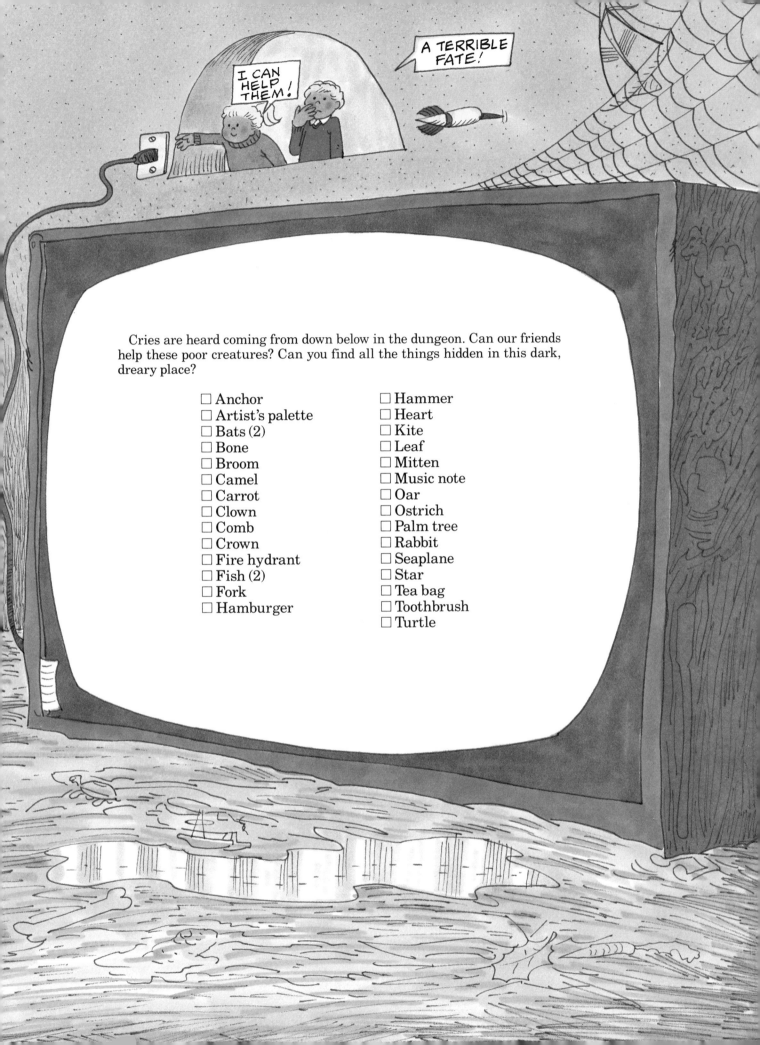

Cries are heard coming from down below in the dungeon. Can our friends help these poor creatures? Can you find all the things hidden in this dark, dreary place?

☐ Anchor
☐ Artist's palette
☐ Bats (2)
☐ Bone
☐ Broom
☐ Camel
☐ Carrot
☐ Clown
☐ Comb
☐ Crown
☐ Fire hydrant
☐ Fish (2)
☐ Fork
☐ Hamburger
☐ Hammer
☐ Heart
☐ Kite
☐ Leaf
☐ Mitten
☐ Music note
☐ Oar
☐ Ostrich
☐ Palm tree
☐ Rabbit
☐ Seaplane
☐ Star
☐ Tea bag
☐ Toothbrush
☐ Turtle

WHAT KIND OF KEYS WON'T OPEN A DOOR?

WHAT ANIMAL DOES A BABY TAKING A BATH RESEMBLE?

WHAT KIND OF DRIVER NEVER GETS A TICKET?

WHAT LETTERS ARE NOT IN THE ALPHABET?

WHAT DOES EVERYONE ALWAYS OVERLOOK?

HOW CAN YOU SPELL MOUSETRAP WITH THREE LETTERS?

WHAT GOES THROUGH THE DOOR, BUT NEVER ENTERS OR LEAVES THE HOUSE?

WHAT KIND OF PET PLAYS THE BEST MUSIC?

WHAT KIND OF A STONE IS A FAKE?

WHAT HAS MANY TEETH BUT CAN'T BITE?

WHAT DOES AN ELEPHANT HAVE THAT NO OTHER ANIMAL HAS?

WHAT KIND OF GIFT IS IT PROPER TO KICK AROUND?

WHAT HAS A THUMB BUT NO FINGERS?

WHAT KIND OF A ROOM IS NEVER PART OF A HOUSE?

WHAT HAS MANY TEETH BUT NO MOUTH?

The jester is so happy to have the TV turned off that he's not only given us the answers to his riddles, he's also hidden the answers in this picture. Can you find them?

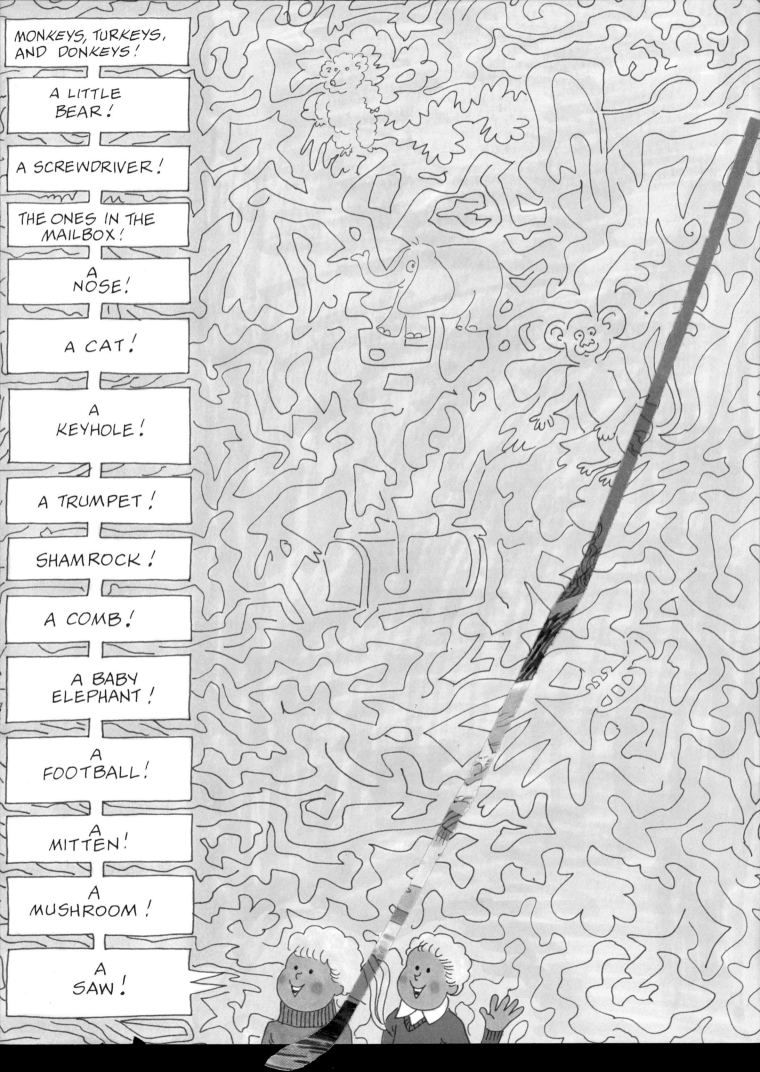

Surprise! Our fearless friends have been invited to a party in their honor. Looks like they're having a creepy, crazy good time!

You too can join in on the fun by finding the following hidden pictures.

☐ Arrows (2)
☐ Bat
☐ Bottle
☐ Cup
☐ Fish
☐ Flower
☐ Fork
☐ Ghosts (2)
☐ Hot dog
☐ Ice skate
☐ Key
☐ Kite
☐ Light bulb
☐ Mitten
☐ Music note

☐ Paintbrush
☐ Pencil
☐ Penguin
☐ Piggy bank
☐ Pinwheel
☐ Rocket
☐ Rocking chair
☐ Roller skate
☐ Seal
☐ Snake
☐ Sock
☐ Spoon
☐ Star
☐ Toothbrush
☐ Truck
☐ Umbrella

I WAS CROWNED PRINCE!

Congratulations! You have survived Creepy Castle! But what crazy gifts have our friends brought home?
See if you can find these peculiar presents. They are hidden in the picture below.

- ☐ Barbell
- ☐ Broken clock
- ☐ Cactus
- ☐ Cat
- ☐ Dog
- ☐ Fire hydrant
- ☐ Flying bat

- ☐ Fountain
- ☐ Heart
- ☐ Ice-cream cone
- ☐ Key
- ☐ Kite
- ☐ Lawn mower
- ☐ Pirate
- ☐ Pizza slice
- ☐ Ring

- ☐ Sailboat
- ☐ Sock
- ☐ Tennis racket
- ☐ Tent
- ☐ Tire
- ☐ TV set
- ☐ Umbrella
- ☐ Yo-yo